LATINOS IN BASEBALL

Ramon Martinez

Jim Gallagher

Mitchell Lane Publishers, Inc.
P.O. Box 200
Childs, MD 21916-0200

LATINOS IN BASEBALL

Tino Martinez	Bobby Bonilla	Roberto Alomar	Pedro Martinez
Moises Alou	Sammy Sosa	Ivan Rodriguez	Bernie Williams
Ramon Martinez	Alex Rodriguez	Vinny Castilla	Manny Ramirez

First Printing
Library of Congress Cataloging-in-Publication Data
Gallagher, Jim, 1969-
        Ramon Martinez / Jim Gallagher.
            p. cm. — (Latinos in Baseball)
        Includes index.
        Summary: A biography of the Dominican-born pitcher who starred for the Los Angeles Dodgers before being signed by the Boston Red Sox in 1999.
        ISBN 1-58415-009-2
        1. Martinez, Ramon, 1968—Juvenile literature. 2. Hispanic American baseball players—Biography—Juvenile literature. [1. Martinez, Ramon, 1968- 2. Baseball players.] I. Title. II Series.
GV865.M356 G34 2000
796.357'092—dc21
[B]   99-057552
About the Author Jim Gallagher is a former newspaper editor and publisher. A graduate of LaSalle University, he lives near Philadelphia with his two dogs. His books include *The Johnstown Flood* (Chelsea House), *Pedro Martinez* (Mitchell Lane), and *Hernando de Soto and the Exploration of Florida* (Chelsea House).
Photo Credits: cover: © 1999 Boston Red Sox; pp. 4, 8 Jon Soohoo/LA Dodgers; p. 18, 21 Andrew Bernstein/LA Dodgers; p. 22 © LA Dodgers; p. 32 Jon Soohoo/LA Dodgers; p. 42 Juan Ocampo/LA Dodgers; p. 53 Brian Snyder/Archive Photos; p. 59 Jon Soohoo/LA Dodgers.
Acknowledgments: This story has been thoroughly researched and checked for accuracy. To the best of our knowledge, it represents a true story. This story has not been authorized nor endorsed by Ramon Martinez or any of his representatives.
Dedication: To my brother Kevin. May the Force be with you.

TABLE OF CONTENTS

CHAPTER ONE
Unhittable

L os Angeles Dodgers manager Tommy Lasorda wasn't sure what to expect when Ramon Martinez took the mound against the Florida Marlins on July 14, 1995.

Martinez had been one of the Dodgers' top pitchers since 1990, the year he became the youngest player in the team's 100-year history to win 20 games in a season. In 1994 he was the team's winningest pitcher, recording a 12-7 record before the season ended because of a baseball strike. Dodger fans had hoped their team's ace pitcher would be at the top of his form in 1995, but Martinez struggled in the early part of the year. By the end of June, he was leading the league in walks and earned runs—two things a pitcher must avoid in order to be successful. During one stretch of three starts, he gave up 20 earned runs. He was allowing over $4^{1}/2$ runs per game, and his record for the season was barely over .500 at 8-6.

Before the game, Lasorda met briefly with Martinez, Los Angeles pitching coach Dave Wallace, and Ralph Avila, the scout who had signed the pitcher when Martinez was a skinny 17-year-old in the Dominican Republic. They discussed his pitching. Privately Lasorda hoped that the pep talk would help to motivate Ramon. His team was slumping and needed its ace pitcher to provide a spark that would turn things around.

There were nearly 31,000 fans in Dodger Stadium as Martinez trotted out to the mound in the top of the first inning. Two weeks earlier, the L.A. fans had booed the pitcher off the mound when he threw poorly in a game against San Diego. In that July 2 contest Ramon had allowed 10 runs in just 4^2/3 innings.

Although there was a smattering of boos when his name was announced, Martinez seemed not to notice. His first warmup pitch, a fastball, exploded into the glove of Dodgers All-Star catcher Mike Piazza. In the dugout Lasorda turned to his pitching coach and said, "Uh-oh." "Right then we knew the old Ramon was back," Wallace said later.

After the umpire shouted "Play ball!," the Dodgers' starter worked quickly. The game was scoreless for the first two and a half innings, as neither Martinez nor Marlins starter John Burkett allowed any hits. In the bottom of the third, however, Burkett got into trouble. John Hollandsworth led off the inning with a double. Burkett then got Martinez to fly out, although this allowed Hollandsworth to advance to third. Lead-off batter Delino DeShields then whiffed for the second out of the inning. But Jose Offerman got the team on the scoreboard—breaking a 21-inning scoreless streak for the Dodgers—with a single that scored Hollandsworth. Piazza then singled to bring Offerman home giving Los Angeles a 2-0 lead.

That lead looked like it might be enough for Martinez, who was mowing down the Florida batters easily. When he held the Marlins hitless in the fourth, fifth, and sixth innings, the fans and sportscasters at the game realized they might just be watching a special performance. One of the most difficult pitching feats is pitching a no-hitter—not allowing any of the opposing team's batters to get a hit. Even more difficult is throwing a perfect game, in which the pitcher does not allow any opposing batter to reach first base, either through a hit, a walk, or an error by a teammate. Martinez had not yet allowed any hits or walks, and the Dodger defense was playing well behind him.

In the top of the fourth inning, DeShields made a fine fielding play to preserve the perfect game. Florida's Chuck Carr, the second batter in the lineup, tried to bunt his way on base. He dropped a perfect bunt down the first-base line, just past the pitcher's mound. DeShields charged the ball and made an off-balance throw to get Carr. "He charged the ball real well and that made the difference," Offerman commented after the game. "If he stayed back a little bit longer, I think [Carr] could have beaten the throw."

In the meantime, the Dodgers scored again in their half of the fourth and struck for four more runs in the sixth to take a 7-0 lead. Having a solid lead was important, Ramon knew. A month and a half earlier, his younger brother Pedro had pitched nine perfect innings for the Montreal Expos. Unfortunately, Montreal couldn't score either, and Pedro lost both his no-hitter and the game in the tenth. Knowing that he had enough runs to win the game, Ramon Martinez could relax and concentrate on making good pitches.

"I'm thinking perfect game, then it got six, seven innings...," Ramon later commented. "Then I'm thinking maybe they're showing this game where [the Expos are] playing. I was watching [Pedro's near no-hitter in June] and I was excited."

Martinez remained perfect through $7^2/3$ innings, until Florida right fielder Tommy Gregg drew a walk

Ramon used his fastball to overpower the Florida hitters.

on a 3-2 pitch. Martinez bore down to strike out the next batter, shortstop Kyle Abbott. Although the chance for a perfect game was gone, the no-hitter was still alive. Martinez was just three outs away.

In the top of the ninth inning, the first batter he faced was Florida slugger Charles Johnson. Throwing fastballs—Martinez did not use his curveball after the third inning—he struck out Johnson. The no-hitter was two outs away.

By now the 30,988 fans in Dodger Stadium, some of whom had booed earlier in the afternoon, were on their feet, cheering for Martinez. Despite their enthusiasm, the pitcher tried to focus on making good pitches. "I heard [the crowd], but I was trying to concentrate on my game," he said of the high noise level in the final inning. "I said [to myself], 'Don't change anything. Don't try to overthrow.'"

The next batter was pinch hitter Jerry Browne, who was hitting .258 for the season. Martinez got him to bounce a hard grounder to second that was easily fielded by DeShields for the second out of the inning. Just one out to go.

As Marlins second baseman Quilvio Veras came to the plate, the normally placid Dodger Stadium crowd was going crazy. Veras, the leadoff hitter, was 0 for 3 on the day, but he was a tough hitter. He worked the count to 2 and 2, fouling off several pitches. Then, on a 90-mph pitch from Martinez, Veras hit a soft fly ball that was easily handled by left fielder Roberto Kelly, ending the game.

Kelly, holding the ball for the final out, ran into the infield, where Martinez's teammates were mobbing the slender pitcher. Ramon's no-hitter was the 22nd in Dodger history, the team's first since 1992, and only the ninth since the Dodgers had moved from Brooklyn to Los Angeles in 1957. And four of those nine had been thrown by one of baseball's all-time greatest pitchers, Sandy Koufax, who had played in the 1960s.

After the game, the Dodger ace was hugged on the mound by Lasorda, while the others who had met briefly with Martinez before the game commented on his great performance.

"He was making quality pitches with his fastball. He established that outside corner down and away and lived there. That's the key to Ramon Martinez's success," said Wallace, the pitching coach. "When he makes those pitches down and away, he's tough."

"I was very excited!" exclaimed Avila, the legendary scout who had managed Martinez when he made the Dominican Republic's national baseball team for the 1984 Olympic Games. "Since the seventh inning, I felt like I was pitching myself. It was really a joy to see Ramon do this, because he was struggling a little bit."

"It was a great feeling," Martinez told reporters afterward. "For many people—the guys, my fans, and my family—I was very excited. Everyone was going crazy, especially people back home. I have pride and I wanted to let people know that I can still pitch. You know something? I think people had forgotten about me."

By the end of the season, no one could forget about Martinez. The no-hitter marked a turning point in his season. He lost just one game in the second half of the year to finish with a 17-7 record and a 3.66 earned run average (ERA). His win total was the third highest in the league, and he was the only pitcher to throw a no-hitter in 1995. Once again, Ramon Martinez had proven that he is one of the best hurlers in baseball.

CHAPTER TWO
Growing Up in the Dominican

Ramon Martinez was born on a small island where baseball is the overriding passion. In fact, nearly 10 percent of major-league players today come from his home country, the Dominican Republic.

The Dominican Republic is located in the Caribbean Sea, to the southeast of Florida. About 7.5 million people live there. It takes up two-thirds of the island of Hispaniola, which it shares with Haiti. The island was discovered in 1492 by Christopher Columbus. Columbus's brother Bartholomew founded its oldest existing city, Santo Domingo, in 1496. It was in a hospital in this city that Ramon was born on March 22, 1968, to Paulino and Laopoldina Martinez. A few days later, the proud parents took their son home to their small farm in Manoguayabo, a small village of about 1,000 residents on the outskirts of Santo Domingo.

Life was not easy in the Dominican Republic when Ramon was growing up. It remains a very poor island even today. There are few good jobs, and the average person makes less than $1,000 a year. Most people work in the sugarcane fields or raise coffee, cocoa, or tobacco. Poverty has forced many people to leave the countryside and move into the cities, especially large urban areas such as Santo Domingo. With the competition for good jobs, thousands of people leave the Dominican Republic each year, seeking better lives in the United States and elsewhere.

The Martinez family was as poor as most of the families in the Dominican Republic. Paulino had a job as a janitor in a local school, and the family owned a two-acre farm on which they eked out a meager living. The small house where Ramon grew up with his parents and five siblings didn't even have indoor plumbing, which meant no inside toilet.

Before starting his family, Paulino Martinez had been a pretty good pitcher for local teams. In fact, he had played with—and held his own against—some of the island's best players, including three brothers who eventually became stars in the major leagues: Felipe, Matty, and Jesus Alou. Felipe Alou, later the manager of the Montreal Expos, once said that Paulino was talented enough to have pitched in the major leagues. "I was too poor to leave the country," Paulino told a reporter in 1998. "When the Giants invited me for a tryout, I didn't have cleats. So I couldn't go to the tryout."

"A lot of people told me how good he was," Ramon later said of his father. "That made me want to play, and to be somebody famous."

As each of his children grew older, Paulino taught them how to play baseball and encouraged them to practice. However, he and Laopoldina could not afford to buy their children equipment to play the game. The Martinez brothers practiced by tossing rolled-up socks or rubber balls, using old broom handles as bats.

"We played baseball all the time, in the streets or wherever," Ramon remembers. "I grew up this way. I was always active, playing with my friends, playing in parks that weren't in very good condition."

While the Martinez brothers' childhoods were mostly happy (despite the constant struggle for money), there were sad moments as well. When Ramon was 13, his parents divorced. While dealing with painful feelings about the divorce himself, Ramon also had to comfort and support his younger brothers. From all accounts, he succeeded. "Our parents cared for us and did a great job instilling values in us," younger brother Pedro, a star pitcher in his own right, told the *Boston Globe* in 1998. "But Ramon is the biggest reason I have gotten where I am. He is the great one in this family."

Ramon poured his excess energy into baseball and spent most of his spare time playing. Among young Dominican baseball players, shortstop is considered the "glamour" position. Ramon, however, always preferred to pitch. He was tall and gangly: he stood over six feet tall and weighed just 100 pounds. But when Ramon pitched, he could blaze the ball past hitters. He could also throw a pretty good curveball—a pitch he learned from his father.

Shortly after Ramon's parents were divorced, a man named Ralph Avila heard about the tall pitcher and came to watch him play. Avila was a scout for the Los Angeles Dodgers. His job was to find talented young players, help them develop, and, if they were good enough, offer them contracts to play baseball for the Dodgers. The players Avila signed would first have to work their way through the minor-league system before achieving the dream of almost every boy in the Dominican Republic—playing in the major leagues.

When Ralph Avila saw the tall, skinny pitcher striking out opposing batters, he was impressed. In 1983 he invited Ramon to a special baseball school sponsored by the Dodgers. At the Campo Las Palmas baseball academy, young players would get instruction on the finer points of playing the game.

At Campo Las Palmas, Ramon was given good practice equipment. He also received instruction from some of the most experienced baseball coaches in the Dominican Republic. For a teenager who had never had much formal coaching, this was a blessing. When Ramon came to Campo Las Palmas, he already knew how to throw hard; now he was being taught how to pitch. "Location is everything," he was told. "It's not how hard you throw it, it's where you throw it. You pitch to where the batter has the least balance."

When his education at Campo Las Palmas was complete, Ramon was invited to pitch with one of the island's top adult baseball teams, the Manoguayabo Braves. It was quite an honor for a teenager who was just starting his first year at Liceo Secundaria Las Americas High School just to be selected. But Ramon became the team's best pitcher.

Even after Ramon left the baseball camp, Ralph Avila kept an eye on the talented young hurler. Avila was the manager of the Dominican Republic's national team that would play in the 1984 Summer Olympic Games in Los Angeles. He chose Ramon to be one of the squad's pitchers. In the Olympics, Ramon would have an opportunity to show the world just how well he could throw a baseball.

CHAPTER THREE
Olympics to Major Leagues

As 16-year-old Ramon Martinez stepped onto the pitcher's mound for the first time in the 1984 Olympics, the crowd cheered. The game was played at Dodger Stadium, the home of the Los Angeles team. Ramon later said that he felt right at home in Dodger Stadium, and that he even told a team scout, "Maybe in four years, I'll be back here pitching."

Ramon pitched three scoreless innings against the team from Taiwan. His performance impressed Dodgers management, who had already heard good things about the young pitcher from Ralph Avila. Three weeks after the Olympics, Ramon was offered a minor-league contract with the team. He signed excitedly, thrilled to be taking his first step toward the major leagues.

But Ramon knew it would not be easy to reach "the Show," as players call the big leagues. Every year, thousands of young and talented baseball players sign professional contracts, but only a handful ever make it to the majors.

Young professional baseball players typically must work their way through four minor-league levels: rookie ball, Class A, Class AA, and Class AAA. Each time a player moves to a new level, he finds the competition is harder. A player may be able to get away with making some mistakes in rookie-league ball; however, by the time he reaches Triple-A, any flaws in his game—

such as an inability to hit the curveball or a lack of control when pitching—will keep that player from ever reaching the majors.

In 1985, Ramon pitched for the Dodgers' rookie-league team in the Dominican Republic. He spent the season as a middle reliever for the Santo Domingo Dodgers. The next year, he was promoted to the Dodgers' Class-A team, the Bakersfield Blaze. The pitching coach for the Blaze, Johnny Podres, had been a star pitcher for the Dodgers during the 1950s and 1960s. Podres had been the hero in 1955 when the Dodgers won their first World Series. He taught Ramon how to throw a change-up—an off-speed pitch that is used to confuse hitters expecting a fastball.

"[Podres] told me I had a great fastball and this would only make it better," Ramon later recalled. "He showed me how to hold the ball with a different grip and how to throw it. I learned right away. It worked from the very beginning."

Although Ramon was able to use the pitch effectively, he had trouble with the hitters that he faced at Class-A. The batters were more patient in the California League than they were in rookie-league ball. Ramon had to throw his pitches over the plate for strikes, giving his opponents better opportunities to hit.

To be a good starting pitcher, a hurler must keep throwing hard into the later innings. However, 18-year-old Ramon began to tire after just four or five innings. Although he was 6 foot 3, he weighed just 135 pounds. He did not have the strength or stamina to succeed.

"When I was in the clubhouse, I used to look at other people and see how skinny I was and feel real bad," Ramon later commented.

Of course, it didn't help that the Bakersfield team was awful. The Blaze lost 104 games. The year was very frustrating for Ramon and his teammates.

When Ramon returned home for the winter, Ralph Avila put him on a high-protein diet. He knew that the young pitcher needed to gain weight and strength in order to make it in professional baseball. By the time Ramon arrived for spring training in 1987, he had gained 17 pounds and was well rested. When the Dodgers' coaches clocked his fastball with a radar gun, they were amazed. He was throwing faster than 90 miles per hour—10 mph higher than he had thrown the season before.

In 1987 Ramon proved that he was one of the bright young stars in the Los Angeles farm system. Playing for the Dodgers' Class-A team in Vero Beach, Florida, Ramon dominated the opposition. He went 16-5, pitched six complete games, and allowed just 41 earned runs in 25 starts.

Ramon started the 1988 season with the Dodgers' Double-A farm team, the San Antonio Missions. He picked up where he had left off in 1987, becoming one of the top pitchers in the Texas League. Ramon's eight victories prompted the team to cut his Double-A season short. In August, he was called up to the major leagues.

The Dodgers were leading the National League West when Ramon arrived, thanks to stars like slugging outfielder Kirk Gibson and pitcher Orel Hershiser, who wound up with a league-best 23-8 record and set a major-league mark by pitching 59 consecutive scoreless innings that season.

In 1988, Ramon helped the Dodgers clinch the National League West title, but he did not pitch in the playoffs that year.

Ramon appeared in his first major-league game on August 13. A little more than two weeks later, he

earned his first big-league win, pitching seven strong innings in a 2-1 victory over the Montreal Expos. Ramon finished the season with the Dodgers, compiling a 1-3 record and a 3.78 ERA in the nine games—six of them starts—that he pitched. His contributions helped Los Angeles win the National League West title; the Dodgers defeated the Mets in seven games for the National League pennant, then took the World Series from the Oakland Athletics, four games to one.

In the spring of 1989, Ramon hoped he could make the Los Angeles squad for the whole year. However, although Martinez had proven that he could get major-league hitters out, Dodgers manager Tommy Lasorda felt the pitcher should get more experience in the minors. After all, he was just 21 years old. Ramon was sent to the Dodgers' Triple-A farm team, the Albuquerque Dukes.

On June 5, 1989, the Dodgers' pitching rotation was exhausted after a series of extra-inning games. The team needed someone to make a spot start and called up Ramon. He made the most of the opportunity, pitching his first career shutout for a Los Angeles victory. Ramon allowed the Atlanta batters just six hits. This excellent performance meant he was ready to remain in Los Angeles full-time, right?

Wrong. The next day, Ramon was sent back down to the minors. It was a great disappointment, but Ramon boarded the bus for Albuquerque.

"I was upset. I thought it was unfair," he later admitted. "I wanted to go home. But I knew that the family needed the money I was sending so that everyone could go to school or play ball or pursue their dreams."

Ramon let his disappointment motivate him. He had shown that he belonged in the major leagues, and he was having little trouble with the hitters in Triple-A ball. Ramon recorded a 10-2 record for Albuquerque and struck out 127 batters in 113 innings. In July, Ramon was brought back up to the Dodgers—this time to stay.

CHAPTER FOUR
Becoming the Dodgers' Ace

R amon had finished the 1989 season with the Dodgers, going 6-4 in 15 appearances. He came to spring training in 1990 with a goal: to stay with the Dodgers for the entire season. The 22-year-old did not expect that by the end of the year, he would be the team's best pitcher.

He started the year quickly, winning his first two starts. But it was not until June 4, when he shut out the Atlanta Braves 6-0, that he began receiving national attention. That night Ramon was practically unhittable: he struck out 18 Braves, tying a team record. The only other Dodger with that many strikeouts in a single game was one of the all-time greats, Hall of Famer Sandy Koufax. After the game, Koufax called Ramon to congratulate him.

"That was a huge experience in my life," Ramon commented later. "It was one of the principal factors in opening the doors to the major leagues for me, because, although I had started here the year before, I still wasn't very well known. But after I tied Sandy Koufax's record with those 18 strikeouts, I began to be recognized."

Ramon continued to pitch well throughout June. He won four games without a defeat during the month and posted a 1.76 ERA. Those numbers were enough for him to be named the National League's Pitcher of the Month. He also was selected to the National League's All-Star team, a great honor for a rookie

Ramon Martinez

pitcher. He was disappointed when his squad lost to the American League team, 2-0.

After the midseason All-Star break, Ramon continued to dominate hitters. By the end of the season, he had struck out 223 batters—just 10 behind NL leader David Cone—in 234 innings. Although Ramon's endurance had been questionable early in his career, he proved that he could go the distance by hurling a major league–leading 12 complete games. He finished the year with a 20-6 record, becoming the youngest Dodger to win 20 games in a season since Ralph Branca in 1947. His victory total was the second highest in the league. Ramon also was second in the league in shutouts with three and posted a scintillating 2.92 ERA.

Ramon established himself as one of the best pitchers in the National League in 1990.

With these great statistics, Ramon finished second in the balloting for the National League's Cy Young Award, which is presented each year to the league's best pitcher. The winner was Pittsburgh Pirates ace Doug Drabek, who had a 22-6 record and a 2.76 ERA.

The emergence of Ramon as one of the league's best pitchers boosted the Dodgers to an 86-76 record. That was good enough for second place in the National

League West, behind only the Cincinnati Reds, who would go on to win the 1990 World Series.

Some pitchers start off their careers with a great season but are less successful the next year. Ramon did not want to be a flash in the pan. He worked hard during the off-season to prepare for his second full year in the majors.

In 1991, the work paid off as Ramon picked up where he had left off the season before. From April 21 to May 24, he reeled off a seven-game winning streak. By the All-Star break, he had a 12-3 record and a 2.45 earned run average. Once again, Ramon was named to the NL's All-Star team. However, this year he did not participate in the game because of a hip injury.

The hip injury was just one sign of the strain that pitching so many innings was placing on Ramon's slender frame. In the second half of the season, he lost some of the velocity on his fastball. Although he finished with 17 wins, the fourth-best total in the league, he had lost 10 games after the All-Star break. His ERA rose to 3.27; his strikeout total dropped to 150 in 220 innings. On the positive side, Ramon threw four shutouts, the second-best total in the league, and pitched six complete games. He also was excited on September 22 when he hit his first major-league home run.

The Dodgers pitched well as a team, leading the league in ERA, and finished second in the NL West again, this time racking up 93 wins and just 69 losses.

But the following year would be much less successful both for Ramon and for the team. The shoulder soreness that had bothered Ramon in the second half of 1991 persisted into the 1992 season. In fact, the pain became so bad that he finally had to stop pitching, and he missed the entire month of September. Ramon was very unhappy with his final statistics: an 8-11 record, a 4.00 earned run average, and 69 walks in the 150 innings that he had pitched—two more than he had allowed in 234 innings in 1990.

"I never had that kind of year," he later said. "It was frustrating. I felt the pain in August and decided to stop. I had pitched with pain before, but not that bad."

The 1992 season was painful for Dodgers fans as well. Their team dropped into last place in the division.

For Ramon, one of the few highlights of 1992 came after he was finished pitching for the year. To help fill the team's pitching void, his younger brother Pedro was called up by the Dodgers in September. The Martinez brothers had come a long way from the Dominican Republic; now they were teammates in the major leagues.

The biggest off-season event for Ramon was his wedding. After the marriage ceremony on January 16, 1993, Ramon and Dorcas Martinez set up their home in the Dominican Republic.

But there was not much time for a honeymoon, since Ramon was working with the Dodgers' pitching coaches. He wanted to change the way that he delivered the ball to the plate. This, Ramon hoped, would reduce the strain on his body.

Ramon was excited when his younger brother Pedro joined the Dodgers during the 1992 season.

The off-season work paid off, and Ramon was able to pitch more than 200 innings in 1993. It was the third time that he had reached that number in his four seasons. However, with the changes in his mechanics, Ramon's control problems intensified. He walked a career-high 104 batters—an average of more than four bases on balls per game. The 104 walks was the highest figure in the league. In Ramon's best season, 1990, his strikeout-to-walk ratio had been 3.33 to 1; in 1993 it was 1.19 to 1.

For the Dodgers, the 1993 season was an improvement. The team did not make the playoffs, finishing third. But they did have an up-and-coming star, a brawny catcher with a strong arm and a good eye in the batter's box named Mike Piazza. The 24-year-old batted .318 with 35 home runs and 118 RBIs to earn Rookie of the Year honors.

As he prepared for the 1994 season, Los Angeles manager Tommy Lasorda made several off-season moves to improve his team so that the Dodgers could return to the playoffs. One of these trades was a deal with the Montreal Expos to bring a young second baseman named Delino Deshields to Los Angeles. In return, the Dodgers sent Pedro Martinez to Montreal, even though the younger Martinez had blossomed in a relief role, with a 10-5 record and a 2.61 ERA in 1993.

Ramon was sorry to hear about the deal. "It made me sad when he was traded," he later said. "But I was also happy because the role he had with the Dodgers was in the bullpen. In Montreal, he [would get] to be a starter."

The older pitcher swallowed his disappointment and dedicated himself to regaining the form he had shown earlier in his career.

In his first outing of the 1994 season, it seemed that the old Ramon might be back. He struck out 10 Florida Marlins on April 7, earning a win. From May 5 to June 13, he won six straight decisions, including complete-game shutouts of St. Louis and Florida.

Behind the revitalized arm of their best pitcher, and with the hitting of Piazza, Eric Karros, and Raul Mondesi—who would be named the 1994 Rookie of the Year—the Dodgers regained the top position in the National League West.

On August 7, Dorcas Martinez gave birth to their first child. She and Ramon named their daughter Doranni. The pitcher returned to the mound four days later and gave the Dodgers a $3^1/2$ game lead in the NL West. His complete-game shutout victory over Cincinnati on August 11 gave him the league lead in shutouts with three.

Unfortunately, that was the last game Ramon would pitch in the 1994 season. In fact, that was the last day that major-league baseball would be played that year. The next day, the Major League Players Association went on strike. The last 52 days of the 1994 season were cancelled, and for the first time since 1904, the World Series was not held.

But the season had been a success for Ramon. He finished with a 12-7 record and was among the league leaders in victories and innings pitched (170). He fanned 119 batters and lowered his walk total to 56. In addition to his three shutouts, he threw four complete games. He also did well at the plate, with 18 hits in 66 appearances for a .273 average to lead all Los Angeles pitchers. The Dodgers' ace was back in top form.

CHAPTER FIVE
A Big Contract

With Ramon's return to form, baseball observers were anticipating that the tall, slim right-hander would dominate in 1995. But the season did not start out that way. In fact, after the first two months of the season, it began to look as if Ramon's strong 1994 had been a fluke.

By the All-Star break, Ramon's record stood at just 8-6. He was leading the league in walks and had allowed more earned runs than any other pitcher in the league.

But his first start after the break, on July 14, was his dominating complete-game no-hitter against the Florida Marlins. This turned Ramon's season around. In the second half of 1995, Ramon went 9-1 with a 2.66 earned run average. He did not lose a game during the last month and a half of the season. His 17 victories were the third-highest figure in the National League and marked the fifth time in his six full seasons that he had reached double figures in wins. Ramon finished fifth in the balloting for the Cy Young Award.

With their ace back in top form, the Dodgers surged ahead in the NL West standings, winning the division for the second straight year. But they were knocked out of the playoffs in the first round by the Cincinnati Reds, who swept the Dodgers in three games.

Even though Ramon was disappointed with the way he had pitched in the postseason—the Reds had torched him for 10 hits and seven runs in four innings in his only playoff start—the Dodgers were very happy with Ramon's fine 1995 season. Ramon's contract with the Dodgers, which had paid him $3.9 million in 1995, expired at the end of the season. The pitcher had the opportunity to become a free agent and entertain lucrative offers from other teams. But he wanted to stay with Los Angeles, and the Dodgers wanted to keep him. They rewarded the star pitcher with a great contract. The deal—in which he would make more than $4.8 million a year in 1996, 1997, and 1998—made him the best-paid Dodger to that point.

"My first choice was the Dodgers," Ramon told the news media afterward. "I was confident we were going to get a deal."

His three-year contract, worth nearly $15 million, also included an option for a fourth year. If the Dodgers were pleased with Ramon's performance and wanted him to remain with the team in 1999, they would have to pay him $5.6 million. If not, they could buy out the final year of his contract for $600,000, and Ramon would be eligible to sign with another team as a free agent.

But free agency was far from his mind as the 1996 season began. Ramon merely wanted to get out on the mound and prove that he was worth the money he was receiving.

The year started slowly for Ramon. Because of a painful hamstring injury, the Dodgers placed him on the disabled list in April 1996. After Ramon recovered from that, he caught the flu, which kept him out of action longer. Following that, he was hurt when a line drive smashed him in the mouth. In all, he missed the first five weeks of the season.

But once Ramon recovered from all his ailments, he picked up where he had left off in 1995. He won his first four starts, extending to 10 games a winning streak that had started August 13, 1995. His return gave Dodgers fans hope as the team battled through the summer with the San Diego Padres and the Colorado Rockies for the NL West title.

The fact that Los Angeles was in contention at all was somewhat amazing, considering the number of top players the team lost to injury during the 1996 season. In addition to Ramon, shortstop Greg Gagne missed the first five weeks of the season because of health problems. A knee injury caused Mike Piazza to miss 12 games in April. In May, Dodgers outfielder Brett Butler was diagnoised with tonsil cancer. He was out for most of the season. And on June 23, longtime Los Angeles manager Tommy Lasorda suffered a mild heart attack. Although Lasorda attempted to return as manager, within a few weeks he realized that he was endangering his life if he stayed on the job. On July 29, after 20 years, Lasorda retired as the team's manager. He was replaced by Bill Russell, a former star shortstop on Lasorda's powerful Dodger teams of the 1970s.

With Russell in charge and Ramon leading the way on the mound, the Dodgers reached the playoffs for the second straight year. The Dodgers actually had a good chance of winning the title outright. Ramon closed strong, recording a 2.74 earned run average and winning seven straight games down the stretch. In fact, the whole team caught fire in August and September, winning 19 of 24 games during one stretch.

On September 20, Ramon threw a complete-game shutout against the Padres. He struck out 12 batters in the Dodgers' 7-0 win. That victory gave Los Angeles an 87-66 record and a $1^1/2$–game lead over San Diego for the division title. Seven of the Dodgers' final nine games were scheduled against the Padres, so the champion would be decided in the last two weeks of the season.

Coming into the final three-game series of the year, the Dodgers were 90-68 and had a two-game lead for the NL West crown. All they needed to do was beat the Padres (with a record of 88-71) one time and Los Angeles would earn the division title. When the Padres won the first two games, the Dodgers' season came down to the final game of the year. Neither team could score, and the game went into extra innings, finally ending when the Padres plated two runs in the 11th to win the game and the division title. San Diego would face Central Division champion St. Louis in the first round.

Because their record was better than all but the division-winning teams, the Dodgers still entered the playoffs as the National League's wild-card team. But they were disappointed at letting the NL West championship slip through their fingers. In the first round of the playoffs, they would have to face the powerful

Atlanta Braves. Atlanta had lead the National League with 96 victories during the regular season. They boasted a formidable offense, with sluggers like Chipper Jones, Ryan Klesko, Fred McGriff, and Marquis Grissom. Their pitching staff, with 1996 Cy Young Award–winner John Smoltz (24-8, 2.94 ERA, 276 Ks) and two other starters who had won Cy Young Awards (Greg Maddux and Tom Glavine), was second only to the Dodgers in team ERA.

Ramon was tabbed to start the first game against Smoltz. Together, the two hurlers put on a pitching clinic. Neither team could manage much offense against the two ace pitchers. Ramon allowed just three hits in eight innings; he gave up a fourth-inning run when a McGriff sacrifice fly scored Grissom. But the Dodgers tied the game, and the score remained 1-1 at the end of nine. Finally, in the bottom of the 10th, Atlanta's Javier Lopez saw a 3-2 pitch he liked from Los Angeles reliever Antonio Asuna. He swung hard and knocked it over the right-field wall for a game-winning home run.

Although the Dodgers played their hearts out, they would never get closer in the best-of-five series. Atlanta won the second game 3-2 behind a strong outing by Maddux, then pounded Hideo Nomo for five runs early in the third game, winning 5-2 behind Glavine. (The Braves then defeated the Cardinals in the League Championship Series to advance to the Fall Classic; they lost the World Series in six games to the New York Yankees.)

Statistically, the 1996 season would turn out to be one of Ramon's best. He finished the year with a

In this 1996 photo of the Martinez family, Ramon is holding his daughter Doranni while his wife Dorcas carries their infant daughter Kisha.

15-6 record for an excellent .714 winning percentage. One of the most important qualities that baseball teams expect from their ace pitchers is the ability to stop losing streaks, and in 1996 Ramon was especially dependable. When he pitched after a Dodgers loss, Ramon allowed opposing teams just 2.38 runs per game, and he won nine of 10 decisions. He pitched $168^2/_3$ innings and struck out 133 batters—including his career milestone 1,000th strikeout on June 18. The victim was Scott Servais of the Chicago Cubs. But of all the events of the 1996 season, three probably stuck in Ramon's mind the most.

The first occurred on June 20, when his wife gave birth to their second child. Ramon and Dorcas named this daughter Kisha.

The second highlight of Ramon's season occurred on August 13, when he won the 100th game of his career. Ramon pitched into the eighth inning, leaving the game with a 6-2 lead. Although the Dodger bullpen gave up three runs, Los Angeles hung on to win 6-5.

After that game, manager Bill Russell and pitching coach Dave Wallace had nothing but praise for the 28-year-old pitcher, whose .592 career winning percentage (100 wins, 69 losses) was one of the best among active National League pitchers.

"He's been the backbone of our pitching staff," Russell said.

Wallace had even more to say about Ramon, reminding reporters about Ramon's dependability when he takes the mound. "Look at the year he's gone through," he said. "He hasn't had that stretch where you get 8-9-10 starts in a row and really get yourself in a rhythm. Still, he's 9-6. Add last year to that, and he's 26-13.

"He's been lost in the shuffle, no question. The biggest thing about him is, he can be wild or not have his best stuff or whatever. You look out there in the seventh or eighth inning, and he has kept you in the ballgame. He always gives you a chance to win."

Ramon himself was fairly low-key after the victory, telling sportswriters that he might drink a glass of champagne to celebrate. "I like what I'm doing," he said. "I just want to be consistent and keep doing what I'm doing." When asked what his next goal was, the pitcher smiled and said, "Win a hundred more."

The final highlight occurred just over two weeks later, when Ramon pitched in one of the more exciting games of his career. For the first time in the major leagues, he was facing his little brother, Pedro. The younger Martinez had blossomed into the ace of the Montreal Expos' staff and had won 11 games—one more than his older brother at that point in the season. It was an important game for both teams as well, as Montreal and Los Angeles were neck and neck in the race for a wild-card playoff spot.

Both Ramon and Pedro were at the top of their respective games, and neither pitcher allowed a run in the first two innings. In the bottom of the third, Ramon induced his little brother to fly out to Los Angeles right fielder Raul Mondesi. But he ran into trouble when the Expos' leadoff man Rondell White singled, then stole second. Rattled, Ramon walked Mike Lansing and Henry Rodriguez to load the bases. Montreal took a 1-0 lead on Ramon's third walk of the inning, to cleanup hitter David Segui, before the Dodgers' ace settled down to retire the next two batters and escape the inning.

The Montreal lead would not last long. With one out in the top of the fourth inning, Dodgers catcher Mike Piazza, who had been selected MVP of the 1996 All-Star Game a few weeks earlier, hit his 31st home run of the season to tie the ballgame. Just two pitches later, Los Angeles first baseman Eric Karros gave his team the lead with a homer over the left-field wall.

That would be all the runs that either team would get, as Los Angeles held on for the 2-1 victory. Pedro had pitched magnificently in defeat. He went the distance, giving up just six hits and the two runs and striking out a career-high 12 batters. But although Ramon had not been as overpowering strikeout-wise with seven, he had allowed just three hits in the eight innings that he pitched.

"I'm very proud of the job that [Pedro] did," Ramon said afterward. "It was a very big challenge for both of us. When he left the mound in the ninth, I made a sign to him to tell him that I love him and that he pitched a great game. Neither of us wanted to give it up and that's the way it should be. I don't feel sorry. I feel very proud of him. It could have been him the winner and me the loser. I have pitched better games and I've been in other good duels, but this is different. It was a big challenge. I just wanted to go out and win and put us back in the wild-card lead. It was a great game, and I'm glad it's over."

Pedro was just as complimentary of his older brother. "He's been a great example to me as a person and as a player my whole life," he said. "I look up to him and he's always been there for me. He taught me how to play baseball and he's taught me about life. He's my idol. It was a little different preparing for this game because I had to go up there thinking that I was going to defeat my brother or that he was going to defeat me. It was hard and it will never be easy if it happens again because it's blood against blood and it's the same blood. I was happy to see the crowd give him such as good hand as well. It's nice to see that they liked him as much as they liked me."

CHAPTER SIX
Battling Injuries

As spring training began for the 1997 season, the Dodgers were once again picked to win the National League West. Los Angeles certainly had the best pitching staff in the division, and one of the best in the majors. Behind Ramon in the rotation were Hideo Nomo, a young Japanese pitcher who had been Rookie of the Year in 1995 and had gone 16-11 in 1996; and Ismael Valdes, a talented right-hander who had posted a 15-7 record in 1996. The fourth starter would be an up-and-coming Korean hurler named Chan Ho Park, who had posted a 5-5 mark and 3.64 ERA in 48 games the previous season.

But the season did not start off so well for Ramon. Even though the Phillies could score just two runs off him in five innings, that would be all they needed. Phillies ace Curt Schilling shut down the Los Angeles offense, allowing just three hits and striking out 11 batters in eight innings as the Dodgers lost 3-0.

The team came back strong, however, and by the time Ramon was credited with his first victory on April 11, a 7-1 win over the Pirates, Los Angeles was tied for first place in the National League West with a 7-3 mark.

Ramon improved to 2-1 on April 18 with a 5-3 win over the Astros in which he struck out seven batters, but by that time the San Francisco Giants had made it a three-team race for the NL West lead. In fact, the Giants (11-3) had taken a one-game lead over Los Angeles and Colorado (both 10-4).

Ramon's worst outing of the year came on April 28, when the Atlanta Braves pummeled him for 11 hits and eight earned runs in five innings. The loss was the Dodgers' seventh in their last eight games and dropped their record to 11-11, five games behind San Francisco and Colorado. The only game Los Angeles won during that span was over the Cardinals, 2-1. Ramon had started that game and pitched seven strong innings, allowing just two hits and striking out nine batters, but he did not figure in the decision.

But the Dodgers seemed to put themselves back together after the loss, winning their next four games.

By May 7, both the team and Ramon seemed to be back on track. Ramon earned his third win of the year by pitching eight strong innings against the Reds and allowing just two runs, and the Dodgers pulled to within two games of division leaders Colorado and San Francisco.

On May 19, Ramon lost a 2-1 heartbreaker to the Expos, dropping his record to 3-3. He pitched well, allowing just five hits and two runs in six innings before being lifted for a pinch hitter in the seventh.

The loss seemed to spark something in the lanky pitcher. He came back May 24 to beat Atlanta 10-3. Ramon pitched a complete game and allowed just two earned runs, outdueling former Cy Young Award–winner Tom Glavine, who was pummeled for eight runs. Six days later, Ramon gave up just one run in seven innings against the Cardinals. The pitcher even helped himself offensively, hitting a double down the left-field line to lead off the sixth inning, then scoring on a single by left fielder Eric Anthony. Unfortunately, that was the only run the Dodgers would get, and St. Louis won the game with two out in the ninth off reliever Darren Hall.

Although Ramon did not figure in that decision, he did pick up his fifth win of the year the next time he took the mound, again allowing just one run in seven innings. He struck out nine batters in the 5-1 win over the NL West–leading San Francisco Giants June 4. Ramon improved to 6-3 and lowered his ERA to 3.08 five days later in an 8-3 win over the Astros. Although he gave up three runs (two earned) in the third inning, two home runs by Todd Zeile powered the Dodgers to the win.

On June 14, the Dodgers suited up for an interleague game with the Seattle Mariners. Seattle was one of the strongest teams in the American League, with an offense that featured sluggers Ken Griffey Jr., Alex Rodriguez, Jay Buhner, and Edgar Martinez. The game turned out to be a slugfest that the Mariners eventually won, 9-8.

The game ended early for Ramon, however. He gave up two home runs in the second inning and allowed three more runs in the third. Although he managed to avoid further damage in the fourth inning, he never came out to the mound in the bottom of the fifth. Instead, Tom Candiotti walked out in relief.

After the game, the Dodgers announced that Ramon had a sore shoulder. Tests revealed that he had a partial tear in his right rotator cuff. On June 23, he was placed on the disabled list.

Ramon was out for more than two months. While he was rehabilitating his arm, the Dodgers continued battling the Giants and Rockies for the division lead. The team was powered by Piazza, who was having the best year of his career (he would finish with a .362 batting average, 40 home runs, and 124 RBIs). By the time Ramon was able to pitch again in late August, he had missed 51 games.

An August 20 game against the Mets was Ramon's first outing after coming off the disabled list. He was hit hard, giving up six runs in two innings, but the game was rained out and did not count. Five days later, Ramon again was on the mound. This time he pitched much better as the Dodgers beat the Pirates 8-2. Ramon gave up single runs in both the first and second innings, but he settled down in the three innings after that. Reliever Mark Guthrie came on in the sixth, throwing four scoreless innings for a save, while Ramon notched his seventh win of the season.

He bettered that outing in his next start, allowing just one run and striking out seven batters in an 11-2 rout of the Seattle Mariners. And after the Dodgers' offense bailed him out in a 7-4 win over the playoff-bound Florida Marlins September 5, Ramon's record for the season stood at 9-3 with a 3.42 ERA.

As the season entered its final weeks, the Dodgers still had a chance to overtake the Giants. However, the team faltered down the stretch. Ramon fell apart with the rest of the team. He was shelled by the Braves,

7-0, on September 10—his first loss since mid-May. Ramon did not figure in the decision in a 7-6 Dodgers win over the St. Louis Cardinals on September 16. He then coughed up a 5-1 lead to Colorado in a 10-5 Los Angeles loss five days later.

With two games remaining in the season, the Dodgers still had a shot at the division title. If they won their final two games and the Giants lost their last two games, Los Angeles would win the National League West. It was Ramon's turn on September 27. As the ace of a pitching staff should, he responded magnificently. He allowed just a single fifth-inning run to the Rockies and fanned six batters in $7^2/3$ innings as the Dodgers won 6-1. The win improved his record to 10-5 on the season and lowered his earned run average to 3.64.

After the game, all the Dodgers could do was root for the San Diego Padres to beat the Giants. But San Francisco was too strong. Their victory over the Padres sealed the NL West crown and ended Los Angeles's hopes of reaching the postseason.

Ramon was disappointed that his team had come up short. But he was very pleased that his brother had blossomed into the best pitcher in the National League. Pedro Martinez had turned in one of the best pitching performances in years. He had finished the season with a 17-8 record that was even more impressive because the Expos were a weak offensive team. Montreal had finished 78-84 and was ranked just 10th in runs scored among the NL's 14 teams. Opposing batters hit just .184 against Pedro, and the 26-year-old had become the 14th pitcher in league history to strike out 300 batters in a season (he finished with 305). He also threw 13 complete games. Pedro was the overwhelming choice for the 1997 National League Cy Young Award.

Ramon and his family attended the November ceremony when the award was presented to Pedro. The presenter was Hall of Famer Juan Marichal, the greatest pitcher ever to come from the Dominican Republic. Then in December, Pedro received the big payoff, signing a $75 million contract with the Boston Red Sox.

During the winter of 1997–98, Ramon and Pedro worked out together in the Dominican Republic six days a week. They would drive to the Olympic Training Center in Santo Domingo, where a tough trainer named Angel Presinol would put them through an intense two-hour workout. After running four to five miles, then stretching, the brothers would do exercises to increase their strength and agility.

Afterward, they would drive home, eat lunch, and work out again for 90 minutes in Ramon's gym. "Six days a week we work, one day we relax," Pedro Martinez told sportswriter Peter Gammons. "Stop working and you go right back where you came from—nothing."

The work paid off. When Ramon arrived at the Dodgers' spring training camp, he felt refreshed and his shoulder felt strong. "I could feel the difference," he said. "My fastball was jumping. I just let it go and I didn't feel anything. My shoulder was like new."

Ramon blew everyone away in the short exhibition season, going 3-0 with a 1.54 earned run average and 19 strikeouts in 23 innings. However, in the Dodgers' season opener against St. Louis, Ramon lasted just $4^2/3$ innings. The damage came on one swing of the bat by Mark McGwire, who blasted a grand slam in the bottom of the fifth inning to give the Cardinals a 4-0 lead. St. Louis went on to win the game 6-0. (For McGwire, the homer off Ramon Martinez was just the first of the record 70 home runs he would hit in 1998).

By the time Ramon's turn in the starting rotation came up again, Los Angeles was in trouble. The Dodgers had lost their first four games of the year and looked to their ace to put them on a winning track. Ramon delivered, taking a no-hitter into the eighth inning against Cincinnati before Eddie Taubensee singled with one out. Ramon retired the first 20 batters before walking Willie Greene with two out in the seventh inning and struck out seven in the 1-0 victory. "That was unbelievable," commented batterymate Mike Piazza. "He was pretty much unhittable."

Ramon had another strong outing on April 10, allowing just four hits and one earned run in eight innings. Offensively, the Dodgers were paced by Mike Piazza, whose grand slam was the biggest blow in the 7-2 victory. Ramon's next scheduled start was April 15, but the game was postponed a day by rain. On April 16, he pitched $6^1/3$ innings against Colorado. Although Ramon did not earn the victory, the Dodgers prevailed in extra innings, 4-3. The win evened the team's record at 7-7.

It was clear that the shoulder injury was not bothering Ramon. "He's throwing the ball as well as I've ever seen," said Dodgers coach and former catcher Mike Scioscia. "It's a testimony to how hard he worked. He has worked so hard to get his strength where it is."

"I've never seen him look better," agreed manager Bill Russell. "He could have ended up with surgery, very easily, but he worked hard all winter. When he came to spring training, he was ready for the start of the season."

Ramon's next outing was a disappointment. He allowed two home runs in a 5-2 loss to the Brewers on April 21 that dropped his season record to 2-2. As usual, he shook off the loss for his next start. On April 26 he allowed just two earned runs in seven innings, striking out eight Chicago Cubs. Although he didn't get credit for the win, as the game again went into extra innings, the Dodgers wound up winning in the 12th, 4-3. This victory capped a three-game sweep of the Cubs and improved Los Angeles's record to 12-11. The Dodgers had moved up from last to second in the National League West, but they were still five games behind division-leading San Diego.

Focused on the hitter: Ramon started the 1998 season strong, and it seemed he had put his shoulder troubles behind him.

Ramon earned his third win of the year on May 2, beating the Pirates 5-4. His next outing, against the Florida Marlins, did not start out well. Ramon gave up four hits and three runs in the bottom of the first. But he bore down and allowed just two scattered hits after that, pitching eight innings in L.A.'s 4-3 win. That snapped a three-game Dodgers losing streak.

On May 12, Ramon earned a no-decision in a 5-3 loss to the Phillies. But the disappointment of that loss was forgotten three days later when, in one of the biggest trades of the decade, the Dodgers traded two of their best players, Mike Piazza and slugging third baseman Todd Zeile, to the Florida Marlins for Gary Sheffield, Charles Johnson, Jim Eisenreich, and Bobby Bonilla. Just a week after that trade, the Marlins sent Piazza to the New York Mets.

Ramon was sorry to see Piazza go. The catcher always seemed to save the game for the Dodgers with a big hit. But one of the new acquisitions, Bobby Bonilla, made himself welcome by driving in the winning run in Ramon's next start. The 6-3 win over the Expos on May 17 improved his record to 5-2.

Ramon picked up his sixth victory with a complete-game, 7-1 win over the Arizona Diamondbacks. It was his first complete game of the year and the 37th of his career. Ramon struck out six batters and did not walk anyone. "I was throwing a lot of strikes, and I had real good location with my pitches," he said afterward. "They were very aggressive, and I was feeling good. I just put the ball where I wanted to, and they were swinging."

In his next start, May 28, Ramon again gave up just one earned run, but this time he had control problems, walking six Cincinnati batters in six innings. The Dodgers prevailed 4-3, but Ramon did not figure in the decision.

On June 2, Los Angeles made another roster move, cutting pitcher Hideo Nomo. A former National League Rookie of the Year, Nomo had been ineffective much of the season. In fact, the whole team seemed to be reeling, falling several games below .500 at 27-30.

By contrast, Ramon remained the team's most effective pitcher. The day after Nomo was dropped from the Dodgers' roster, Ramon threw seven strong innings in a 7-4 win over the Cardinals. This time, Mark McGwire did not play, and the rest of the St. Louis lineup could manage just five hits and one earned run off the Los Angeles ace. The victory improved Ramon's record to 7-2 and lowered his earned run average to 2.70. He was tied for second in the league with seven wins, behind Greg Maddux and Jason Schmidt, who had eight apiece.

Disturbingly, however, Ramon's shoulder was starting to feel tender. His continued control problems—Ramon had walked five batters in the win over the Cards—reflected the pain he was feeling in his right arm. In his next start, June 8, Ramon walked five more batters and hit one. The Dodgers lost that interleague game 7-3 and fell $8^1/2$ games behind the streaking Padres. Ramon had allowed all seven runs, although only four of them were earned, in taking his third loss of the season.

On June 14, Ramon was pitching fairly well against Colorado in the fifth inning when he felt a sharp pain in his shoulder. It hurt too much to continue, and he had to leave the game. (It was tied 1-1 when Ramon walked off the mound; the Dodgers eventually lost in the 12th inning, 3-2.)

Dr. Frank Jobe, the Dodgers' team doctor, examined Ramon's shoulder and gave him the bad news: his rotator cuff was torn and would need to be surgically repaired. Ramon was placed on the disabled list and surgery was scheduled right away. Ramon was finished for the 1998 season, and doctors told him he probably wouldn't pitch for a long time. There was even a possibility that he would never be able to pitch again in the major leagues.

On June 30, Dr. Jobe and Dr. Lewis Yocum performed the surgery on Ramon's shoulder at Centinela Hospital Medical Center in Los Angeles.

"We feel we did a good repair," Dr. Jobe said after completing the procedure. "It'll take about a year before he can pitch in a game. I'd be inclined to think that he'll be just like he was before." He also told reporters that the pitcher would have to change his throwing style in order to make a complete recovery.

The day after the surgery, Ramon began to work out. He started with simple exercises designed to strengthen his shoulder and to keep the rest of his body in shape. Ramon knew there was no guarantee that he would ever pitch in the major leagues again. It would be five months before he could even throw a baseball. But Ramon wanted to do everything he could to make certain he would once again stand on the pitcher's mound of a major-league stadium.

Unfortunately, he soon learned that if he did pitch again, it might not be for the Dodgers. In March 1998 the team had been sold by the O'Malley family, which had owned it for many years. The new owner was Rupert Murdoch's Fox Group, and during the season the Dodgers organization had been rocked by numerous personnel moves. One was the blockbuster trade of Mike Piazza. Another came on June 21 when manager Bill Russell was replaced by Glenn Hoffman, and longtime Dodgers general manager Fred Claire was fired and replaced by Tommy Lasorda. Both of those appointments were on an interim basis. On September 11, Kevin Malone was hired as the team's new general manager, and he hired Davey Johnson to manage the Dodgers. In December, pitcher Kevin Brown, a free agent who had starred for the Padres, signed the richest contract in baseball history to that date, a seven-year deal worth $105 million.

In October the Dodgers announced that they would not pick up the option year on Ramon's contract. The team had decided that an injured pitcher who was scheduled to make $5.6 million in 1999 was not a good gamble, so they paid the $600,000 buyout.

Ramon knew that he could file as a free agent, meaning that any team could bid for his services. However, he decided not to file. Of the 137 players eligible, Ramon was one of just two players who did not file for free agency. (The other, Lenny Dykstra, retired.) Ramon wanted to work on rehabbing his shoulder, and he hoped the Dodgers, or some other organization, would offer him a new contract if he were able to come back.

Because it is so difficult to find quality major-league starting pitchers, several teams were willing to take a chance on Ramon Martinez. When Ramon received interest from the Boston Red Sox, he decided he wanted to reunite with his brother Pedro. In March 1999, he signed a two-year deal with the Red Sox. The contract also included an option for the 2001 season. Ramon was satisfied with the pact, which would pay him about $24 million if he stayed with the team all three seasons.

"If he comes around like we hope, he will have an impact," commented Boston general manager Dan Duquette. "He's a good leader, too."

Pedro Martinez was ecstatic that his brother had joined the team. In the Red Sox's 99-year history, Pedro and Ramon were the first brothers to pitch for the team at the same time. Boston's second baseman, Jose Offerman, was also pleased. Offerman had played with Ramon in Los Angeles from 1990 to 1995. "Ramon is a good man and a good teammate," he told the Associated Press.

CHAPTER SEVEN
Comeback

On September 1, 1999, Red Sox manager Jimmy Williams told reporters that Ramon Martinez would make his first start for Boston the next day. Because it would be Ramon's first major-league outing in more than a year, he would be lifted after throwing approximately 85 pitches. Boston knuckleballer Tim Wakefield, who had spent time both in the starting rotation and as the team's closer, would relieve Martinez, Williams explained.

Ramon had worked hard to get his right arm back into shape. Recovering from rotator-cuff surgery is a long, hard process. Many pitchers never make it back. But even when he struggled in outings against minor-league hitters, Ramon focused on making it back to the majors.

"When I start[ed] my rehab, when I start[ed] my throwing, that was the hardest part because there was a lot of pain, sore days where I [said], 'I probably am not going to make it,'" Ramon admitted in a *Boston Globe* article. "There was a lot of [soreness], but I never stopped. I never g[a]ve up."

His return was timed perfectly. With the Red Sox in the middle of a hot playoff race against the New York Yankees, Oakland Athletics, and Toronto Blue Jays, fans were excited about Ramon's potential. They knew that strong pitching down the stretch was necessary for the Sox to clinch a playoff spot. Boston pitching coach

Joe Kerrigan reminded reporters not to expect too much in Ramon Martinez's first start. He noted how difficult it is for any pitcher to recover from shoulder surgery.

"There are always doubts when someone has a major injury," Kerrigan told *The Boston Globe*. "But knowing the character of the man, I believed he could do it. We've created a spot for him in the rotation. That's how much we think of him. But after this start, we'll have to evaluate and see how he feels."

Ramon was "confident," he told news reporters. "It's been a long time since I've been out there, but I just look at it as another game."

More than 31,000 fans showed up at Fenway Park on September 4 to see Ramon face off against the Kansas City Royals. The adrenaline was pumping in the top of the first inning. Ramon needed just eight pitches, including a strikeout of Carlos Beltran, to set the Royals down. "I was focused and excited," he said later. "I said, 'Let's go right at them.'"

Unfortunately, in the next few innings Ramon seemed to lose his focus. He gave up a leadoff single, walked the next two batters to load the bases, then gave up a run when he accidentally plunked Joe Vitiello with a fastball. But Ramon bore down to get out the next three Kansas City batters, striking out Sal Fasano, inducing Jed Hansen to foul out, and whiffing Johnny Damon.

Ramon gave up another run in the third inning, then was lifted in the fourth after allowing a two-run homer that put the Royals up 4-0. The Sox dropped the game 4-2; Ramon ended up taking the loss.

Afterward, Ramon and his coaches felt generally positive about the pitcher's first outing in more than a year. "I wasn't disappointed," Ramon said. "I was disappointed with the result, a loss, but it was a good outing for me. I don't feel any kind of pain. The only problem I had was that I walked a couple of guys and that was it. But it was exciting. I liked the way I was out there.

"I just want to get back out there and pitch a better game than I did today," he added. "But it was my first game in over a year and there were a lot of things on my mind out there. I feel good I was able to go back out there and pitch."

Manager Jimmy Williams was pleased as well. "His arm was free," Williams said. "He had a real good change-up. You could see the quality was there."

However, Ramon had not shown enough to break into the Red Sox rotation. He would have to wait until Williams needed a spot starter to have a chance to pitch again.

He did not have to wait long. On September 14 he got the call to start against the Cleveland Indians. This time Ramon pitched better. He lasted $4^2/3$ innings, struck out five batters, and allowed three runs. Boston won easily, 14-3, and although Ramon did not get credit for the decision, he was pleased to pitch again.

On September 25, Ramon got a chance to start his third game of the season. Boston pitcher Pat Rapp had to leave the team because his wife, who was having a difficult pregnancy, gave birth to their son prematurely. Ramon made the most of his opportunity against the Baltimore Orioles. He threw seven strong innings, allowing just four hits, walking no batters, and giving up just one run in a 4-1 victory—his first since June 3, 1998. The win also snapped Boston's three-game losing streak, keeping the team in front of Oakland in the race for a wild-card playoff spot.

"There were a lot of moments in which I thought I wasn't going to pitch this year," an excited Ramon Martinez told *The Boston Globe* after the game. "I felt and touched a sore shoulder, and I said to myself I might not be able to make it. But I kept working.

"Before the first game I pitched, there were a lot of questions. There is a lot of excitement and a lot of expectations. I lost, but that game allowed me to see how [it was going to be] when I came back and pitched and how I was going to react. After the second start, I had more confidence. Today was much better. I knew we had the pressure that we had to win. We'd lost three straight."

Two days later, Pedro Martinez took the ball for the Sox and ensured at least a tie for the wild-card playoff spot by pitching Boston over the Orioles 5-3. The Red Sox's 6-2 win over the Chicago White Sox in the first game of a doubleheader on September 28 ensured that the Red Sox would return to the playoffs for the second straight year.

Ramon was tabbed to pitch in the Sox's second-to-last game of the season, on October 2. He shut out the Orioles over six innings, allowing just two hits, as

Teammates again: Ramon and Pedro in the Boston dugout, 1999.

Boston won 8-0. His brother Pedro came out in the seventh to pitch an inning in relief—the first time that Ramon and Pedro had pitched together in the same game for the same team since September 13, 1993.

Afterward, Ramon downplayed speculation that he might be one of the Red Sox starters in the playoffs. "I was concentrating on pitching good, not making the playoff roster," he said. "It is a matter of time for me. I feel confident I can get better."

Pedro, however, was more exuberant. "I can't describe my happiness for my brother in words," he said. "It is a plus to have him doing well. We were not counting on him for the playoffs, but now we are."

The Red Sox finished the season with a 94-68 record, four games behind the Yankees (98-64), who had posted the best record in the league. Under the new playoff rules adopted in 1995, in the first round the division champion with the best record plays the wild-card team, and the other two division winners play each other. However, because the Yankees and Red Sox were in the same division, Boston would instead face the division-winner with the second-best record. The Cleveland Indians would not be any easier than the Yankees, though. In fact, Cleveland had knocked the Sox out of the playoffs in the first round the year before.

Fans in Boston were excited. The last time the Red Sox had made two consecutive postseason appearances was back in 1915–16.

There was a lot of talk about the powerhouse Boston teams from early in the century; most of it centered around a talented young pitcher who had won 18 games for the Red Sox in 1915, 23 games in 1916, and 24 games in 1917. In the 1918 season, the pitcher won 13 games; he also played 75 games in the outfield and batted .300 with 11 home runs, which tied for the league lead. That fall, the Red Sox won the World Series on the strength of his left arm. He won three games, and pitched a Series-record $29^2/3$ straight scoreless innings.

The next year, he spent even more time in the outfield, and set a new league record with 29 home runs. But despite this, the Red Sox had finished in sixth place in 1919. In the off-season, team owner Harry Frazee sold his star player's contract to the New York Yankees for $125,000, plus a large loan.

In Yankee pinstripes, this man—George Herman "Babe" Ruth—would go on to make his mark as the game's greatest player. Before his arrival, the Yankees had never won a championship; with Babe Ruth they reached the World Series seven times and won four. New York would remain the century's most dominant baseball team. And the Red Sox, after winning the Series three times in five years with Ruth, have not won a championship since. The long-suffering Boston fans attribute the drought to Ruth's departure, calling it "the curse of the Bambino."

Ramon, Pedro, and the rest of the team hoped to break that streak by reaching, and winning, the last World Series of the 1900s. To get there, they would have to knock off Cleveland, then beat either the hated

Yankees or their first-round opponents, the Texas Rangers.

A few days before the playoffs began, Jimmy Williams announced his starting rotation for the playoffs. Ramon would be the number three starter, after Pedro and another former Cy Young Award–winner, Bret Saberhagen.

The Indians had a potent offense, and they quickly showed why they had been one of the league's best teams for nearly a decade. Pedro started the first game but had to leave early because of a strained back muscle. The Indians ended up winning 3-2. Then Cleveland followed up by shelling Saberhagen in the next game, en route to an 11-1 rout. The Red Sox were just one game away from playoff elimination as Ramon Martinez took the mound.

The tall Dominican has almost always pitched well in big games. The night of October 9, 1999, was no exception. He pitched $5^2/_3$ strong innings, giving up just two runs, and Boston won 9-3.

With that victory, Boston's bats seemed to come alive. In the next game, the Red Sox erupted for a playoff-record 24 hits and 23 runs, evening the series with a 23-7 victory. And fittingly, Pedro Martinez was the hero in the pivotal fifth game. Although a few days earlier he had not even been able to throw the ball softly without feeling pain in his back, he was well enough to come out in relief of Saberhagen, who again was hit hard. Pedro finished the game, pitching six no-hit innings, and the Red Sox emerged as the winners, 12-8.

While there was celebration in the clubhouse as Boston rejoiced in its first playoff series win since 1986, the team knew its next opponent would be even tougher. The New York Yankees, who had beaten the Rangers, were the defending World Series champions. Even though they had not duplicated their incredible 1998 season, in which the Yankees set an American League record with 114 wins, New York did have a potent lineup and a solid pitching staff. The series took on extra emotion because the Yankees had been Boston's most hated rival since before the days of Babe Ruth.

The Red Sox took an early lead in the first game, scoring three times in the first two innings. But the Yankees battled back, tying the game in the seventh and forcing extra innings. In the 10th, New York won it on a Bernie Williams home run, 4-3.

In the second game of the series, Ramon took the mound for the Red Sox. He hoped to play the same stopper role that he had in the Cleveland series and help the Sox tie things against the Yankees. Then the league championship series would shift to friendly Fenway Park for the next three games. Although he had never faced the Yankees in his career, the slender right-hander had encountered some of the players, including star outfielder Paul O'Neill, and he had watched the other Yankee hitters closely during the first game.

Ramon worked his way out of trouble several times during the first six innings. Although he gave up a fourth-inning home run to Tino Martinez, the Red

Sox came back to take a 2-1 lead in the top of the next inning on Nomar Garciaparra's two-run homer.

But things turned ugly in the bottom of the seventh. Ricky Ledee led off the inning with a walk and moved to second on a sacrifice fly by Scott Brosius. Martinez got the second out of the inning by inducing Joe Girardi to hit a shallow pop fly to the outfield, but the next batter, Chuck Knoblauch, rapped a double down the left-field line to drive home Ledee with the tying run.

At that point, Martinez left the game to the cheers of the crowd. He had thrown 120 pitches, his highest pitch count of the season. Reliever Tom Gordon, the team's former closer who was also coming back from an arm injury, was brought in to try to stop the bleeding. Unfortunately, he walked the next batter, Derek Jeter, and let Knoblauch steal third. Jimmy Williams then called for a left-handed reliever, Rheal Cormier, to replace Gordon and face the dangerous Paul O'Neill. In the regular season, O'Neill, a .300 hitter, had batted just .190 against left-handers. However, he delivered a base hit to drive home Knoblauch with the go-ahead run.

After walking the Yankees' best clutch hitter, Bernie Williams, Cormier got out of the inning by causing Tino Martinez to ground out to first, but the damage had been done. The Yankees led 3-2. The Red Sox would not be able to mount a comeback.

Afterward, Ramon Martinez was disappointed. Although he had pitched well, he was credited with all three Yankee runs and took the loss. "I didn't want to come out in my situation in the game, but I had to come out," he said. "It was an exciting game and I wanted to keep going."

With his arm troubles corrected by surgery, Ramon Martinez will work hard to remain one of the best pitchers in baseball.

Although the Red Sox would win the next game on the arm of Pedro Martinez, who struck out 12 Yankees in seven innings in the 13-1 victory, New York took the fourth and fifth games to close out Boston's hopes.

But Ramon's remarkable comeback at the end of the 1999 season marked him as a man to watch in Boston's rotation the next year. Not only had he come through as a leader on the field, he also had grown into a leadership role in the clubhouse. He was sure to be a factor in the Red Sox's plans for 2000.

"The only word I can think of to capture Ramon is 'special,'" Boston manager Jimmy Williams said. "This is a very special man."

Anyone who watches Ramon Martinez persevere in his pursuit of excellence would have to agree with that sentiment.

CHRONOLOGY

1968   Born to Paulino and Laopoldina Martinez in Santo Domingo, Dominican Republic, on March 22

1983   Participates in Campo Las Palmas at the invitation of Dodgers scout Ralph Avila

1984   Pitches in the Summer Olympic Games in Los Angeles for the Dominican Republic team; signs contract with the Los Angeles Dodgers

1985   Pitches for the Santo Domingo Dodgers, a rookie-league team

1986   Learns how to throw a change-up from former Dodgers pitching great Johnny Podres while pitching for the Class-A Bakersfield Blaze

1987   Has breakthrough minor-league season, winning 16 games for the Vero Beach Dodgers

1988   Called up to the major leagues by the Dodgers in August; makes first appearance on August 13; defeats Montreal Expos in his first start, 2-1; Dodgers win the World Series

1989   Pitches first shutout, against the Atlanta Braves; finishes with a 6-4 record and 3.18 ERA in 15 games

1990   Finishes second in balloting for the National League's Cy Young Award after recording 20-6 record, 2.92 ERA, and 223 strikeouts

1991   Named to the National League All-Star Team for the second consecutive year

1992   Ends season early due to shoulder injury; younger brother Pedro is signed by the Dodgers

1993   Marries Dorcas Martinez on January 16; is disappointed when Pedro is traded to the Montreal Expos at the end of the season

1994   Dorcas gives birth to a daughter, Doranni, on August 7; totals 12-7 record with a league-leading three shutouts before the season is cut short by a strike

CHRONOLOGY CONT'D

1995   Pitches no-hitter on July 14; finishes among the league leaders in victories with 17 and helps Dodgers win the National League West title; agrees to three-year deal worth nearly $15 million

1996   Records 1,000th strikeout on June 18; Dorcas gives birth to a daughter, Kisha, on June 20; wins 100th game on August 13; helps Dodgers get into playoffs, then participates in pitching duel in the first postseason game against the Atlanta Braves

1997   Wins 10 games despite missing more than two months with a partial tear in his rotator cuff; brother Pedro wins National League Cy Young Award

1998   Gets off to 7-3 start before rotator cuff injury ends season; undergoes surgery on June 30; Dodgers decline to pick up option year on his contract

1999   Signs two-year contract with the Boston Red Sox, with option for third year; works to recover from arm surgery; makes first start for Red Sox on September 4; helps Boston defeat Cleveland in the first round of the American League playoffs

MAJOR LEAGUE STATS

ar	Team	ERA	W	L	G	IP	H	R	ER	BB	K	Avg
88	LA	3.79	1	3	9	35.2	27	17	15	22	23	.216
89	LA	3.19	6	4	15	98.2	79	39	35	41	89	.219
90	LA	2.92	20	6	33	234.1	191	89	76	67	223	.221
91	LA	3.27	17	13	33	220.1	190	89	80	69	150	.229
92	LA	4.00	8	11	25	150.2	141	82	67	69	101	.245
93	LA	3.44	10	12	32	211.2	202	88	81	104	127	.255
94	LA	3.97	12	7	24	170	160	83	75	56	119	.249
95	LA	3.66	17	7	30	206.1	176	95	84	81	138	.231
96	LA	3.42	15	6	28	168.2	153	76	64	86	133	.245
97	LA	3.64	10	5	22	133.2	123	64	54	68	120	.243
98	LA	2.83	7	3	15	101.2	76	41	32	41	91	.206
99	Bos	3.05	2	1	4	20.2	14	8	7	8	15	.192
tals		3.44	125	78	270	1752.1	1532	771	670	712	1329	.235

INDEX